Moggy the Milk and the Runaway Float

Stephen Peart

Illustrated by
Penny Dann

Hamish Hamilton
London

For Katy, Robert and Oliver

HAMISH HAMILTON CHILDREN'S BOOKS

Published by the Penguin Group
27 Wrights Lane, London W8 5TZ, England
Viking Penguin Inc, 40 West 23rd Street, New York, New York 10010, U.S.A.
Penguin Books Australia Ltd, Ringwood, Victoria, Australia
Penguin Books Canada Ltd, 2801 John Street, Markham, Ontario, Canada L3R 1B4
Penguin Books (N.Z.) Ltd, 182–190 Wairau Road, Auckland 10, New Zealand

Penguin Books Ltd, Registered Offices: Harmondsworth, Middlesex, England

First published in Great Britain 1989 by
Hamish Hamilton Children's Books
Copyright © 1989 by Stephen Peart
Illustrated by Penny Dann
1 3 5 7 9 10 8 6 4 2

British Library Cataloguing in Publication Data
CIP data for this book is
available from the British Library

ISBN 0–241–12664–9

Typeset in 16/22 pt Plantin by Wyvern Typesetting Ltd, Bristol
Printed in Hong Kong by Imago Publishing

Moggy the Milk lay in his bed dreaming about the excitement to come.

Tomorrow was the day of the big surprise party!

In his dream he could see his boss,
Norman, gazing at the lovely spread
before him.

"Do you think she'll like it?" asked
his daughter, Nathalie.

"Oh yes," replied Norman, "and
those cream cakes are the best you have
ever made."

"Wasn't the surprise party for Miss Squirrel a good idea of Moggy's?" Nathalie smiled.

Moggy felt himself blush and a little wave of pride washed over him.

All at once his lovely dream was
shattered by the ringing of his
telephone. Before he could even lift
the receiver to his ear, he heard a loud
voice at the other end, thundering,
"M-O-G-G-Y!"

Moggy sprang up like a jack-in-the-box.

"Norman, is that you? What's the matter?" Moggy muttered, still half asleep.

"What's the matter?" bellowed Norman. "You're only an hour late for work! Today is the day of the big surprise party for Miss Squirrel at the school. We've got lots to do."

Moggy got dressed as fast as he could. He grabbed his cap and apron and jumped into his wellington boots. Two paws went into one boot, and over he fell with a loud crash.

"I do hope it's not going to be one of those days," thought Moggy, as he struggled to sort himself out.

In no time, Moggy was racing down his garden path. He swung around on the gatepost – which he always did to save time if he was late – and suddenly collided with Sergeant Basil Bloodhound coming the other way.

"And where are you off to in such a hurry?" enquired the Sergeant.

"I'm late for work," gulped Moggy, "and today is a very special day."

"Well, do be more careful," warned the kind, old policeman, "and take care with that milk-float."

Moggy arrived at the dairy to find Norman pacing up and down.

"Sorry I'm late," he panted.

"I'll forgive you this time," said Norman. "Now come along, there's a lot of work to do."

Just then Moggy saw a large cream trifle. He was just about to dip in his paw for a quick taste when he noticed Norman glaring at him.

"I was only going to count the cherries around the top," Moggy mumbled.

"Just help me load the float," groaned Norman, whose face was beginning to turn as purple as a raspberry yoghurt. "You still have your round to do, before delivering the cakes to the school."

They carefully loaded the food and cream cakes onto the float, taking care to surround them with crates of milk for protection. Then Moggy was on his way.

Moggy worked hard all morning
without a break.

"At last," he sighed, as he pulled up
outside Lookout Garage, where his
friend Monty Mole worked. "Wait until
I tell Monty about my day."

"Morning, Moggy," shouted a voice that seemed to come from nowhere.

Moggy turned to see Monty appear from beneath a large pile of old wheels and exhaust pipes.

"How are things going for the big surprise party?" asked Monty.

"Oh, everything's ready," sighed Moggy. "But I've had an awful start to the day."

"Never mind," said his friend. "I'll put the kettle on and you can tell me all about it."

Monty soon appeared from the shed with two steaming cups of tea and they settled down for a chat.

Suddenly Monty looked up.

"Where's your float, Moggy?" he asked.

"Just outside the gate," replied Moggy, spinning round to have a look. "Galloping goldtops! It's gone!"

The two friends ran over to where the float had stood.

"Monty, look! It's rolling down the hill!" cried Moggy. "We must catch it. The party food is on there."

"Don't worry!" said Monty, running to the garage.

Moggy felt his heart sink as Monty wheeled out a very old-looking motorbike.

"We'll never catch it on that thing," declared Moggy.

"Thing indeed," snapped Monty, feeling rather hurt.

"I'm sorry," said Moggy. "Just hurry!"

Moggy watched as his friend tried to start the bike. It seemed hopeless. He could see the float was already gathering speed and heading for some roadworks. Suddenly the bike roared into life.

"Quick, jump on!" cried Monty.

Monty leapt onto the bike and they raced out of the yard.

They had almost caught up with the float at the roadworks when Moggy had an idea.

"Try and get alongside, Monty, and I'll leap off into the cab," he shouted.

"Right!" cried Monty.

Just then however, Colonel and Mrs Granville Goat came riding round the corner on their tandem.

"Look out!" shouted Moggy.

Monty swerved just in time to miss them, but the float crashed into some bollards and shot through a gateway into a field.

As Moggy and Monty watched the
float bump and jerk over the grass, the
Colonel came striding over with a face
like thunder.

"What do you two think you're
doing?" he roared.

Before Moggy could explain, Monty
suddenly cried, "Look!"

The float was heading straight for
Belinda Hare, the vet, who was
attending to Old Blossom, one of
Farmer Brock's prize cows.

"Look out!" they all shouted at the top of their voices. Belinda looked up just in time as the float sped past, through another gate and back onto the road again.

"After it!" shouted Moggy, as the float continued on its journey, ripping down a 'For Sale' sign in its path, that Mr Freddie Fox had just put up.

"It's heading for the dairy," yelled Monty.

"Faster!" urged Moggy. "I must get on board."

Within moments they had caught up with the float and Moggy bravely leapt into the cab and grabbed the wheel. He pulled hard and the float swerved past the dairy gates into Farmer Brock's yard. It crashed into a huge haystack, where a group of school children on a visit to the farm stood with their teacher, Miss Squirrel.

Norman and Nathalie came running up.
As Nathalie began to explain to Miss
Squirrel about the surprise party they'd
planned for her, a big cheer came from
the children. Nathalie turned to see
Moggy appear at the top of the
haystack.

"What a day!" Moggy sighed. "But
at least the cakes and food are safe, so
let's get on with the party!"